The Mardi Gras Unmasking

Ruan Willow

This is a work of fiction. Similarities to real people, places, or events are entirely coincidental.

First Edition.

Edited by
Dark Raven Edits.

Copyright 2021 Ruan Willow

ISBN: 978-1638482130

Written by Ruan Willow.

Published by Pink Infinity Publishing, 2021.

For all lovers who give to, sacrifice for, enjoy, and love their lovers in all their exquisite and intricate kinky ever-evolving layers.

Table of Contents

Chapter One 4

Chapter Two..10

Chapter Three 23

Chapter Four 35

Chapter Five 47

Chapter Six 62

Chapter Seven...77

Chapter Eight..92

About the Author 105

Other books: 107

Chapter One

I crush myself against the wall by the window like a half-naked thief. My heart jitters out hasty beats. I nudge the curtain aside and peer into the dark night, looking for people having sex on the street. I scan the street up and down. There must be someone fucking.

A crowd of people stroll under the streetlight. They yell. Music blares from somewhere. Sparkling masks and shiny beads catch rays from the streetlights and make people glow. I spy two people deep kissing. Their combined silhouette thrashes against the light streaming from the magic store's window. A lone saxophone sweetly drones from a nearby balcony. Around the bend, many are likely seeking the sexy temptations blooming on Bourbon Street. If only I could see them too, or join in.

The pulled curtain has lit the room a bit. I glance at the door to see if he's coming back yet before I adjust my pale-pink camisole. I bite my lip. I want the lace at the top to lay across my breasts evenly over my mounds while still showing generous cleavage. Must look sexy for Dane, using every fiber of my lust and my body and the sheer openness of my mind. Hell yes. I draw in a deep breath and slowly release it as I cup my breasts and squeeze. I'm so ready for this sexual mystery of his to roll out. My evil grin rages in the darkness. Only he knows my secrets. Such a good Dom Dane is turning out to be for me.

I finger the feathers flowing off the top of my mask, taking extra time to feel up the pink one that matches my camisole as if it's somehow different. I play with a large blonde curl that has flopped onto my breast. Today was a good hair day. The door clicks and my breath catches. The air chokes me as I grasp the wall with my fingertips.

Should I hide better? I love it when he finds me, his hard cock swinging, eyes full of lust, strong hands overpowering me, picking me up like I'm a doll. Wearing this mask, camisole, and thong all night at his request. Now I'm a skeptical little girl with an impatient, swollen clit. And oh yes, I'm ready to be rubbed enough by Daddy Sir to spill a flood.

"Kara? You here, baby?" Dane asks in his tender voice.

I let out a sigh as butterflies claim my gut. "Yes, I'm here." I step out from behind the armoire, the tallest feathers on my mask bouncing above my forehead as I creep forward in baby steps.

"Oh good." He moves quickly across the room with his long-legged stride. "You've followed my instructions." His voice is thick with approval.

Mmmm. I like it.

He grabs both of my biceps and squeezes, lifting me slightly off the ground, enough to make me tippy-toed as he brushes his full lips along mine.

He smashes my tits to him by pressing hard on my back. I gasp. Seriously. I can't move. I blink and blink. The strength of his hands melts me. My gut feels like warm putty. I open my mouth to speak but can't. I force out the words. "Claim me, Daddy."

He pries my lips open with his tongue and fondles mine.

His cock is a rock against my tummy. And I want it in me right fucking now.

He tugs my thong up my ass crack with a devilish grin. "There. All better." Even in this dim light, his eyes twinkle.

"I want you," I whisper into his mouth. "Please, fuck me. I need you in me now. I wanna be your Mardi Gras whore."

His devil mask covers most of his face, but leaves his beautiful pouty mouth visible, his strong chin, the horns covering his waves of lush brown hair. "I so want those lips and

Ruan Willow

your tongue on my clit." I run my finger over his wet lips, our mutual desire almost palpable. The new song coming from the living room makes me want to dance. I shimmy my shoulders against his strong grip.

He steps back and releases his hold, then he tips up his mask to show me his face unencumbered.

I get his full naughty grin in tune with his lusty eyes. Delicious. "Fuck me," I whisper.

"Oh, you'll be my whore, alright. And get my lips all over you. That and more. I just need to go tend to a few of the guys. They wanted me to make them a martini. I'm a bartender slut at the moment. Then I'm all yours." He replaces the mask and hops back from me as I lunge for him. He walks to the window and peeks out, then pulls the curtains closed snug darkening the room once more.

He whips his fingers in the air and closes them quickly. "I'm doing everybody. I'm the master bartender with a perpetual boner." He chuckles but sobers when I frown. "Sorry, I'll be back in no time, kitten. I just wanted to check on you. You're being a very good girl, coming in here and staying just as I asked you to do. I noticed you followed the plan to the very

The Mardi Gras Unmasking

second even. That's my good girl. You'll be rewarded for listening to Sir. Daddy is quite pleased with you."

I shove my lower lip out in a pout, but my smile slips out. "But I was having fun at the party, and it's still going on, so I really want to go out there. Or you just stay here and fuck me. They can make their own drinks." I grab for him.

He jerks back. "Don't you worry, baby girl, I'm going to take care of all your needs. I want this night for you because you want it." He cocks his head at me, a finger tap to his chin. "You being in here at the start of it all is imperative."

"Only I don't know what the 'it' is." I hook my thumbs in the front of my thong and sag my shoulders, but the thrill of not knowing also excites me. My pulse races. My clit blissfully twitches. I can't wait. If I clap, he will punish me.

"Now, none of that moping. I won't be gone for more than five minutes, and then I'll be back to ravage you senseless, wring you out with fucking until you are limp and a useless treasure for me to covet in my arms." He leans over to pet my hair. "Now, remember the rules?"

"Yes, yes. I do. Please hurry back. My pussy is soup-gushy, and she wants to spit on your hard cock." I run my thumb down my groin. "Fuck I'm horny."

Ruan Willow

"Yes, kitten. Now get on the bed, ass up, face in the pillow, and wait." He turns away.

I ogle his round, firm ass as he heads out the door. "Always ass up," I mutter in barely a whisper as I climb onto the bed. I curl up on my side, wistfully listening to the laughter and music wafting through the crack in the door as he shuts it behind him. I want to be in both places. My heart pounds. A tear wells up in my throat. Don't cry. Don't cry. I've had way too much wine. Chill Kara. I will get him to myself soon.

Chapter Two

This night is something he wants for me that I need. Hmmmm. What could he have planned? I'm dying to know. I just need his cock in me, that's what I need, pounding me to the submission of multiple orgasms loaded with many contractions each. Yes, please. I slip my finger past the soft fabric of my thong and into my pussy. I'm so wet and I haven't even been touched on my pussy by anyone but myself in hours. Hmpf. I stick my lip out. I sit here waiting for some cock from the man who promised to always give me some when I wanted it, for life. So where is he? I slam my fist onto the bed. He'd call me a brat for that and slap my ass. No doubt. But that's why I do it. And I'll do it again and again. I chuckle.

I twirl a spiral curl around my finger as a tremor travels through me. I'd better get my ass up or I'm going to get spanked for not following the plan, for real. But...I wanna get spanked, but...I kinda don't. I naughty smile as I nestle my face into the soft pillow barely in time as the door clicks open. Ha! I made it

Ruan Willow

into position in time. Whew. That was too close. My heart pounds as I pant.

He's upon me fast, like a damn panther. His beer scent is strong. He slides his hand along my right hip.

I jerk to the left, only to be reined in by his hand on my left hip. I grin against the soft pillow. It's always so delicious when he fixes my position.

He warns me with two rapid grunts.

I'm not going to do it. I'm gonna test ya. I grin as I lower my hips, making me slip out of his large hands.

He grips my hips harder and pulls me back up into position.

His correction makes me naughty grin again. Fuck. I want him.

I hold my breath, waiting for the slap for being an "insolent brat", as I bite my smile back. I tense as his right hand leaves my hip. I want to lean to the side, but I wait.

The Mardi Gras Unmasking

I wince. OMG. Slow down, heart… I might have a panic attack. My chest is heaving, pressing my breasts into the bed with each inhale as I arch my back. This sucks ass. I don't want to be still. His grip on my left hip tightens. I gasp.

Here it comes …

Smack! Smack! Smack! Smack! Smack!

He delivers wild hard spanks that burn my ass cheeks instantly. My face jerks forward into the pillow with each hit. I whimper out right along with each skin slap. My clit twitches, my pussy flares. That skin on skin smack sound … fuck that's hot!

He smacks my ass again. Hard.

That's it. Punish me, Daddy. I curl against the comfort of the bed.

He utters a long low guttural growl like he's getting satisfied.

Mmmm. I love that.

I widen my eyes as my mouth gapes open. Wow. This must be what he means by 'it', delving further into BDSM, something new. Do I like this? I don't know yet. But yes. Of course, such thoughts sure as fuck make me come hard when I use my toys alone. I need to accept his punishment. I can do it. I will.

He migrates that spanking hand now gently, softly down my butt cheek, his touch so tender, careful. He rubs his palm all around the wetness between my legs, coating himself with my excess of juices. Then he jerks his hand away. He smacks my ass again twice with my wetness all over it.

Mmmm. So naughty, Dane. Whoa. Fuck. He never fails to stun and surprise me. But, damn, he's never done that before.

I whimper, murmuring my sounds as I writhe against the soft bed.

He spanks me again.

My pussy flares as does my asshole as the spank vibration travels along my pelvis. My eyes widen as I suck my lip into my mouth. I'm a bad girl for liking this. What is wrong with me? I'm

The Mardi Gras Unmasking

some kind of sicko. No. Damn my guilt tarnishing liking this… I gotta let that go. My skin begs for his touch, this I know — harsh and soft, all. I don't know why, but I want it. I have no clue why I like the nasty shit, all I know is it makes me come. Maybe it's because of what Papa did. My face heats. I admit it. I want Dane to dominate me, my lust something like that Pavlov's dog stuff or something. Will I hide my eyes from him when next our gazes meet? No. We love each other. I can give him control. I want to. I squeeze the soft comforter in between my hands; it squishes too easily. I sigh. Dane, I surrender.

I wiggle my ass, readying for another smack as I sneak a glance back at him. I should frown, right? I can't let my evil laughter spill; that would only bring on his wrath. Which I kinda want, though. That's when his passion peaks and I swoon the hardest. I so want him to rage fuck me, pound me hard into my climax. I know right when, and how, I will provoke him. I sorta want to crawl under this comforter and hide. Pick one, dammit Kara!

As he leans forward, the silver sequins along the eyeholes of the mask barely flicker, catching the light from somewhere, and dim out where it meets the black sequins at the corners. It makes him look evil.

I hide my eyes back into the pillow as his tongue laps at my asshole, making me squirm. I can imagine what we must look like together if someone were to suddenly open the door, and the image wets my pussy. I glance at the door. I want that to happen. Someone watching us. Oh please, yes.

The tip of his tongue delves into the dips that pucker down deep between my cheeks. As he wiggles his tongue, only the pointy end of it enters me. I fight a full shudder. Truly cringe-worthy, Dane. He drags his chest over my ass cheeks in a hug. I try to shrink away, my skin still stinging. Painful but pleasurable, our bodies mold together. We just fit. Always.

My clit twitches as I imagine his hard nipples sliding across my buttocks. And then he does it. Whoa. Fucking mind reader tonight, Dane. If only he knew I call him Dane in my head instead of Daddy Sir. I suppress my chuckle. What he doesn't know won't hurt him. I get to be naughty just for me. And no one needs to know.

The Mardi Gras Unmasking

He plants a kiss on each of my burning ass cheeks. Ah, such tender kisses make my love for him swell.

I sigh as my pussy further wets. What a man. Fuck. I want him to touch my pussy. So fucking bad. So. This is him revealing new fantasies for me. Maybe? I can handle this, Dane. I'm a big girl. Fetishes don't scare me. I cock my head against the pillow. How in the hell does his tongue feel pointier? He easily snaked it right into my hole, cuz his tongue is blunt. It shouldn't feel like this! That last glass of wine is fucking with my head pretty damn good right now. I'm a moron. I bite my lips together to keep my giggle in.

After a particularly embarrassing twenty-second tongue-ass fuck, he backs away. How does that even possibly taste good? I hold my breath. I refuse to move. That one might take some getting used to. I release the breath of air out of my lungs, nice and slow, Kara. Nice and slow. He runs his tongue along my labia lips, briefly visits my clit, then travels back to my anus. All around my world, huh, Dane?

Yesterday, he fucked my ass with my new skinny butt plug. I'm still acclimating to something in my ass, and now there's his tongue. But isn't today about me? He told me earlier that today would be my sexual fantasy dream come true. What could that dream truly be for me? I'm positive it's not an ass-tongue fuck. As we slip into this new Dom/sub lifestyle, he seems to be able to read me like a book though, yet I'm a foreign language to my own self. Clueless as fuck. But he's helping me explore my deepest desires, supporting me, and I love him for it. Yeah. He loves me. I'm a lucky girl.

He gathers my hair into a ponytail and gives it a tug … of course, he wants a blowjob.

I'd love my tongue on his cock for a bit. I smile at him, even though it's dark, arching my left eyebrow. I slip off the bed, using the edge to steady me. Shivers travel my body. I shake my head so my hair lands on my back, brushing my bare skin in light wispy tickles before it stills. Never sucked cock with a mask on before. I suck back a laugh. Yeah, that would have ruined the moment. Pins and needles all over, I'm so excited I can't stand it.

He saunters slowly around the bed toward me like he's zoned in, deliciously stalking me. I delight in being his prey. His white skin catches the bit of light streaming from between the

The Mardi Gras Unmasking

curtains, somehow they've parted a tiny bit, making his skin glow whiter. The sequined mask on his face catches a rare stream of light here and there, reflecting light as he moves. His cock is a solid straight stick as usual; a gleam of wetness shines on his cockhead as he nears me.

I want your yummy boner, Dane. My eyes follow it. Damn, so hypnotic the way it swings back and forth slightly, like a log on a chain.

The light coming from the streetlamp disappears, the lightbulb probably having just died. I guess. But now it's so dark again. I can barely see his cock, and I can't even see his nice abs at all.

I can barely make out him moving his hands together and apart like he's clapping but not touching, his hands moving several times over his cock as I drop to kneel in front of him. I place my head between his separated hands, and he shoves his fingers into my curls. I open my mouth, practically drool spilling out the corners of my mouth for him, but he lifts me to stand, hooks his fingers under the hem of my camisole and lifts it over my head as I raise my arms.

Ah. Yes. He always wants me naked to blow him.

My breasts flop out and he grunts with satisfaction as he gropes them.

I squirm delightfully at his touch.

He then slips his thumbs under my thong above my ass and slides them down my tender cheeks.

He's gentle, but I still wince, the effects of his harsh spanking still plaguing my skin. I sigh as he drags his thumbs down my ass crack as he strips me. Each touch sets me more on fire.

Mmmm. Make me bare, baby. I breathe in rapid pants.

He lets go and my thong falls to the floor.

I'm fully naked now except for my mask and my toe rings. His clever gifts the evening he asked me to marry him. He promised a better ring to come. I finger the palm side of my wedding ring with my thumb. He certainly delivered.

He groans like it's a complaint, which is amusing rather than annoying, that boyish charm.

The Mardi Gras Unmasking

I refrain from the urge to shake my head, though. So impatient, when I've been the one waiting on him for like forever in here while he mixes the whole party cocktails. I tip my head to the right as he groans again. Hmmm…it sounds deeper than his normal groan, his passion deepening his voice in his throat, no doubt. I remain frozen, awaiting his instruction.

He holds my ears firmly between his big hands as he guides me down to kneel in front of him again, back where I started. I grab his engorged penis with my hands and gently stroke him, then take him into my mouth. Being drunk helps me take more of his cockhead and shaft into my mouth without gagging. He's already applied coconut oil to his shaft, so my hands and lips slip smoothly over his boner. I caress him with my mouth, enjoying his soft groans as I ride up with my tongue flush against his hardness, popping my lips off at the top. His taut front vein feels less prominent against my fingers as I take the head of his cock fully into my mouth again. The dark must be messing with my perceptions. Well, I'm drunk, no doubt, which is also making me ready to explore, savor the layers of his manhood. I can't wait for what's next.

I moan with him in my mouth.

Ruan Willow

He whispers in a strained voice, "Yes, make sound. So good. Love it when you hum."

I'm loving his new hot pleasure sounds.

Shut up, Kara, and obey! Focus. "Mmmmmm. Mmmmmmmm," I mutter with my mouth full of cock.

"Fuck," he murmurs in a husky voice.

I suck him as I stroke, taking in the rich musk of his skin, which also smells like a citrus aroma mixed with a tangy cologne. I didn't even know he owned a cologne like that.

He moves himself in and out of my mouth as he takes control of the blowjob.

I let him, but as I grasp his firm toned thighs, his cock chokes me, and I fall back.

He drives me into the bed for two thrusts of his cock down my throat, but I violently gag and squirm away from him.

This, I'm not a fan of.

The Mardi Gras Unmasking

I sit on the floor and let his cock fall out of my mouth. He will most likely spank me for punishment, but I don't care. Bring it. I'm not scared of him. Do your worst.

I snuggle up to his thighs as I lick the length of his cock.

He strokes my hair and my cheek, down the back of my head to my neck.

I nuzzle to worship and plant love kisses on his cock as he caresses my upper back, his touch so comforting. I rub my lips all over his hardness and swipe my tongue over the tip to catch any pre-cum drips.

He suppresses a chuckle as I giggle and rub his hard-on all over my face, ending with another suck of his swollen head.

Chapter Three

He taps me on the top of the head. Oh goody, my favorite, missionary position.

I stand. I'm giddy and dizzy at once as he hands me a glass of wine. I take a few sips and hand it back to him. I smile, my eyes partly closed. A great top off to my tipsiness indeed. I lie back down on the bed and he goes for my feet.

He licks at my toes, his tongue slow and savoring.

Wow, toe-licking, that's something else he's never done before.

He takes my big toe into his mouth and sucks it. The wet warmth sends erotic waves up my leg, ending in a clit jolt. Mmmm. Wow.

I gasp as his tongue fully conforms to my toe and strokes it like he does when he sucks my tits, like he's milking it.

"Mmmm … fuck," I whisper. Damn, toe sucking is way more erotic and sensual than I imagined. I wiggle. I'm loving his new moves.

He makes his way down my foot, sucking each toe and running the tip of his tongue between each at the base.

The Mardi Gras Unmasking

I wiggle the toes on my other foot.

Like I gave him the idea, he sucks those next, one by one, as he moans and loudly slurps.

He licks my sole.

I giggle, squirm away. "Tickles," I whisper. I yank my foot away, but he holds me still and licks me again as I thrash about and screech, "Oh my Gawd, stop! That tickles like crazy!"

He releases a hearty, almost foreign chuckle. He runs his tongue up my right shin, up to my thigh.

My heart is pounding. I can't quite place it. His voice sounds so different right now.

Chill, Kara. I'm sure he's just drunk. That's why he's doing these new things and sounds like that. He probably did more shots with the guys before coming in here, and the liquor is affecting his voice. My social butterfly caves to do a shot with any buddy of his in a heartbeat. I twitch against his firm tongue snaking its way along my skin. Whatever he sounds like, it doesn't matter, he's doing me all the right ways.

He grabs my thighs and pulls me to the edge of the bed until my ass cheeks just barely hang off.

"Mmmm, fuck me. Yeah. Fuck me hard." I stare into the darkness at the ceiling, trying to focus on seeing the bumps to

Ruan Willow

calm myself down. I yearn to jump up, push him onto the bed, and sink onto his long shaft. But this is his show, so I can't steal his lead.

The music blares on the other side of the door in my living room. People are talking, hooting, yelling.

Oh, I love this song! It comes at the perfect time for the perfect distraction. Hmm. I so want to run out there and dance now, but yet I'm enjoying him, so no chance of that happening. He's all mine now. Plus, I'd be in for major discipline if I did that. But that could be a good thing ...

"Relax, sweetheart," he says in a husky booze-soaked voice again.

I nod and reach up for the glass of wine.

He rushes to grab it for me, to give me what I want.

I sit up so I can take a sip. My bare pussy presses the plush blanket as I bend upwards slightly to claim my drink. I wiggle with pleasure after I swallow. "I need to refresh my buzz a bit more, perhaps." I giggle.

I chug most of the glass and hand it back to him, then lay down fully flat on the bed. I'm a good, obedient girl. The comforter is extra soft and smells fresh, like some sort of flower. Hibiscus or something, our new laundry detergent.

The Mardi Gras Unmasking

He pops open a cap—something in his hands.

The scent of lavender hits me. Oh, my favorite. Yay!

He squirts the lotion on my stomach and spreads it all around my skin with his strong, firm hand strokes.

I love it when he savors my skin like this. Thank you, Dane.

I let out a sigh as my muscles melt under his pressing hands. The lovely aroma of lavender is so relaxing.

His fingers slither down to my pussy mound and he spreads open my lips, starting at my cleft. I let a soft moan out. He licks up in a wide swipe of my pussy, which he repeats five times, like a tongue pet, from my anus to my clit. The licks send shock waves out from my clit as I moan and wiggle. Oh yes, time to pamper me.

My Dane, you really are such a sweet and giving man, not selfish like Max. I wouldn't ever have married Max. No way in hell. Thank goodness I said no. He was all about him coming, it was just a bonus if I did not a priority like it is with you. What a dreadful lifetime of sex that would have been. Thank goodness you showed up in the same coffee shop as me that day. They say a person can't know who they will marry. Well, that's not true. I knew I'd marry you, Dane, from the first moment I laid eyes on

Ruan Willow

you, your broad shoulders stretching out an orange hoodie, magnificent lush brown hair popping out of the hood, eyes that suggested you were about to laugh heartily at a joke at any given moment. You were mine, and I was yours, right from that very first encounter.

He open mouth sucks my clit, his mouth fully, deliciously suctioned to me like those suckerfish sliding around on those aquarium walls in the lobby at work. I suppress a snicker. Not an image to savor. I writhe, grinding myself against his hot sucking mouth while moaning, grabbing at the loose fabric of the bedding at my sides, squeezing it in fistfuls. I gasp as he sucks my clit hard and his two fingers enter my vagina. He knows my body, pleasing me as if he can read my mind.

He fingerfucks me faster than the beat of the song blaring out in the living room. He rides my pussy with his hand. Wet sloshy sounds of his pumping into me dance with his movements. He's going to make me come now.

I'm totally his putty. Love that he's obsessed with making me spill cum. I'm a very lucky woman.

"Mmmm," I moan out, his hand giving me even more pleasure.

The Mardi Gras Unmasking

He crawls up me as I slide farther back up the bed. He takes my right nipple in his mouth. He sucks it deep inside, attempting to deep throat my tit.

I drop my mouth open in a sigh as he rubs his tongue against my nipple, letting it slowly slip out. I want as much of him inside me as possible right now.

He visits my other nipple and nibbles enough where it almost becomes a bite, and I yell out. He crawls back down to eat me out again, his tongue riding my swollen clit. It's driving me up the hill of my climax fast.

He backs away from me, and I try to make out his form in the dark. He looks distorted, like he's just a bit taller and a bit thinner. Nah, I'm just drunk, laugh out loud! The darkness is tricking me. Now I'm seeing things. A buzz roars, a familiar buzz. Ah! My favorite wand. I can't wait for that deliciously hard clit pressure. A shake is building in my pelvis. I moan louder to let him know that I love his plan. He's about to make me come.

My body lurches at the first touchdown of the throbbing wand to my clit.

He presses the buzzing toy to my clit even harder while still fingering me.

Ruan Willow

I'm moaning and he's murmuring something I can't make out above the wand's buzz and the music.

He says it louder, "Yes, yes, yes, baby girl, come for me. Yes, yes, yes."

The familiar pressure point near my belly button flares, as if someone is pressing my tummy from the outside, but it's coming from the inside of me. I fall down the climax to full body twitches as my clitoris contracts my vagina in a series of pulses I can't seem to count, but I round ten at least. I can't stop my body. My legs bend, and my arms curl in toward my torso. The orgasm rules me as I hunch my back, causing my abdomen to scrunch up and my toes to curl, my lips purse, my eyelids droop as I groan out the end of my climax. He loves how I look like I'm possessed when I come. My body relaxes. Euphoria settles upon me. I slow grin. My limbs fall to the bed and my panting slows down.

Simply whoa. And wow. That was damn intense as all hell.

He lines up his cock at my pussy lips and rubs the tip against all of my wetness. His light touch makes my clit flare, but I still my body, I need to resist the urge to lurch away. This will surely pass quickly. My pelvis recoils as he presses his cock

The Mardi Gras Unmasking

to my clit. But, nonetheless, I'm not going to complain as he penetrates me. I want him in me way too much to protest. My whole pussy throbs, my legs too as he enters me.

I yell out as his hard-on fully penetrates me. Gripping his biceps, I dig my fingernails into his firm skin.

He grunts. Thrusts himself into me slowly, deeply as the slosh sounds announce to the silence how wet I am.

Mmmm, love that sound.

I'm mounting an orgasm again quickly as he speeds up his pumping, our skin slapping together in lush smacks. Being so close to my climax, my clit rages herself with electric jolts spreading into my abdomen as he begins to pound me like an enraged animal, the fast hard pounding I love. I moan and whimper, fuck yes, I'm nearing the deliciousness of another orgasm.

He stops and withdraws from me, then pokes on my hip bones with his fingertips. I know that was coming.

I flip to my stomach and raise up on all fours, my ass up higher than my head as I bend my knees, scooting them up closer to my hips, my head hovering closer to the bed.

He grabs a wad of my hair and presses his boner into my pussy from behind. Mmmm love it when he fucks me doggy.

Ruan Willow

I moan and whimper as he pulls my hair to ram himself into me. My eyes roll as his other hand lays firm on my hip. I raise my torso off the bed and force my elbows into the mattress. I'll help with the doggy fuck of me. And I know it pleases him, so I do it. My mouth falls open as I whimper, drool leaks out. I swipe it with my tongue. Fuck, I want his fast pounds! The faster and the harder he thrusts into me, the better.

"Yeah. Yeah. Yeah," I beg.

My ass cheeks shake and jiggle as his abdomen slams into them, deliciously body-spanking my sore buns. He fires off a barrage of hard thrusts. A burgeoning scream threatens in my throat, and a luscious tingle, that oh so sweet contrast of pain and pleasure on repeat, is raising me up as I climb to my climax once again. Please don't stop, Sir Daddy, Daddy Sir.

"Mmmm. Fuck me Daddy Sir," I murmur. "Yes. Yes. Yes. Don't stop. Don't stop."

He pumps into me so fast and I soar into another orgasm. Crashing hard into coming, my body quivering itself into the shakes.

I let my whimpers leak out into the silent room as he continues to pound me through that agonizing sensitive phase once more.

The Mardi Gras Unmasking

He lets out a low man-growl.

Primal as fuck. Pride at making you about to come hard swells in me, in this delicious euphoria I'm swimming in. This is why I married you, Dane. This and how you make banana pancakes and vanilla flavored coffee on Saturdays, with cheese sticks on the side. You just know me. You get me. You touch me deep inside where I can touch myself.

"Fuck, yes. Mmmm, fuck," he murmurs in a voice that sounds somehow deeper, like he has a cold. "Uh, fuck." He shoves himself in me with several more grunts. His cock luscious rubbing my inside walls, slamming my clit.

His strong rapid thrusts cause me to squeeze his cock with my pussy.

He lets out a deep moan.

I groan as he slides out of me. Damn, I want more, I shouldn't have squeezed. I bite my lip. What a sexual glutton vixen I am. So, yeah, I'm a nympho. I let a chuckle slip.

The slosh sounds of him hand-pumping his cock fast fills the air, sounding so super wet. I really want his cum on me, in me, somewhere.

His satisfied sounds peel out of his mouth as he comes, further stirring my want for him to fuck me again. "Fuck!"

Ruan Willow

Then silence. He must have ejaculated on the towel on the bed because I felt no hot splat, but I smell the evidence of his ejaculation. Hmmm. How odd.

The silence is freaking me out. My nerves are just shit from coming twice so quickly. I hold my head and curl up on my side.

He clears his throat, sounding like himself again, to my huge relief. He massages my feet, moves slowly up my shins, my thighs, taking time to kiss each inner thigh. I gasp as he places a peck on my mound. "Okay, kitten. I'll be back to fuck you more. Going to refill our drinks, baby girl. You are so, so, so good, baby. So good. Good girl to come two times. You were simply perfect." He rubs my shin again and I blink in the darkness, looking back at him as he says, "I want you to really enjoy this. Sweetheart, close your eyes while I leave so you can rest for round two. Want you fully recovered."

Feeling like I'm in a comfy sweet bath, I nod my intent to obey as the door clicks shut. He's already fully ravaged me within an inch of my life. Anything more he offers will just be the icing. His praise warms my heart and I want more of it. I open my eyes. Rising up on my elbows, I glance at the clock. It's

33

The Mardi Gras Unmasking

one o'clock in the morning and he claims he's going to fuck me again? I shake my head.

"Wow. No whiskey dick going on with him," I say with a chuckle. "Thank Gawd."

Chapter Four

I touch my pussy and it's sloshy wet, the distinctly erotic smell of him teasing me, still wafting off the towel at my side. I search around for my wand and hover it above my clit, but I resist. Because he says he's coming right back. Geez. I really am ridiculous for wanting another orgasm already. This wine is making me horny as fuck.

I roll to my side. My mind spins.

I can't wait for tomorrow. Friends for lunch being it's Sunday and we have the time. So excited! Hot Chaud Pain, one of my favorite restaurants two streets over, one we found a year ago on our first foray from our apartment after our wedding day into downtown New Orleans for dinner. And what a day that was! Good food. Tall hurricane drinks in curvy pink plastic glasses with orange wedges and straws appropriately placed with their tips still encased in paper. A simple gift of dark chocolates to open before we enjoyed dinner. Street bands belted out tunes as we walked along afterward, bellies about bursting. Then we came home and fucked like banshees. Sex is our passion, and it ties us together hard.

The Mardi Gras Unmasking

I shrug and squeal. Beignets in the morning! Because it's Sunday, and coffee, and Dane. I'm a lucky, lucky woman. I almost clap but …

The door opens a crack and I quickly avert my face. Before the door clicks shut, I dare to peek before he gets swallowed up in the darkness of the room. His devil mask catching a tiny bit of the light from the living room in the silver sequins. The mask feathers are flopping as he walks. Well, he moves with more of a strut. People in our living room are in constant chatter, laughing, mingling without me or him. I'm in seclusion from my own party for the sake of a fuck fest. Wait … that's awesome! Ha! But most unusual indeed. Bring it on.

"Look at the far wall still, sweetheart, so I can surprise you. Close your eyes, open only when I tell you."

"Okay, lover, always trust you." I sigh and hug myself. Oh, such a yummy feeling when I'm about to get royally fucked. "I can't wait for what we will do next." I giggle. "Will it be new things again?" Certainly, I'm an eager slut for him.

"Oh, yes, lover baby girl. I will do new things to you. A sexual smorgasbord of new stuff. This is your special night I planned for you and I can't wait to shove myself in you." He

Ruan Willow

gives me a hug, leaving his scent lingering in the air as he withdraws. "I'm gonna fuck you hard. Just like you want."

His words elicit a spray of butterflies to fill my gut. Raging lust, an indulgent splurge of want freshly blasts my aura. I'm oozing libido, his libido feeding my lust.

"I want you."

"And you will have me. Hey, I filled your wine glass up too. Do you need anything else, babe?"

"No. I'm perfect." I can't shake the euphoria.

"Oh, yes you are. You are sexy as hell, hotter than hell. Now keep your eyes closed and turn your head back straight like you would be staring at the ceiling, but keep your eyes closed tight. It's dark, but still, do as I say. I know you will listen to me without a blindfold, won't you, baby girl?" A command rather than a question. That tone of his voice makes me drip.

Yeah. I get it. I'm not a doorknob. I silently giggle. "Yes, Daddy Sir. I will keep my eyes closed and wait for your delicious touch."

"That's my good girl. Keep them sealed. I mean it." Dane draws a finger from my thigh down to my ankle, sending proper chills all around my body. "Your skin is so soft."

The Mardi Gras Unmasking

I draw in a breath, my lust tingling along my skin like a breath, meandering my desire while enlarging it. I scramble for some semblance of control over myself. I need to concentrate. "Are the guests doing okay?"

"Perfect. Don't you worry about them at all. Focus on you. I'm tending to them, and then when I'm in here, Henry is manning up to be substitute host for me while I pleasure you. So, no worries to ruin this, okay?"

"Okay. But I kind of feel bad I'm in here. Like I'm ignoring them all." Though this is way too luscious of a fucking fantasy to stop on their account. I smile. What must they all think of me staying in the room and Dane coming and going?

"No. You were out there all evening. Now it's about you. Satisfying your sexual needs, baby girl. That and beyond. I want you a wet-soaked quivering sexual slutty mess, drunk on orgasms by the end of this night. So much so that you can't walk, talk, or do anything but shiver yourself to sleep amid a million endorphins swirling inside your body. Gonna push you to a record number of orgasms."

"Wow!" His words tickle every part of me inside with a giant clit twitch on top. "Yummy. I can't wait to feel it all."

"You are on your way, no?"

Ruan Willow

"Yes. Oh, yes I am." I run my hands over my smooth thighs as I shift my legs about.

"Okay, baby girl, keep those peepers closed as I pleasure you like the sex goddess queen you are." He pauses, his voice pregnant with something more. "Get ready."

I giggle and squirm on the bed as my heart ramps up to beat herself against my chest wall like she's trying to break out of me.

"I'm more than ready," I declare, my face melting into a smile. I wait, agonizingly so.

His first touch is to my left cheek, which makes me jump.

I so totally expected him to touch my pussy or tits first after all that previous foreplay. Well played, Dane.

He drags his finger lightly down my cheek and runs it along my closed lips, left to right. He draws his finger back to the left but stops at the middle of my mouth, presses in, and rides my tongue with it. I hungrily suck.

His touch is so tender it relaxes me instantly.

"Mmmmm," he says. He drags his saliva-soaked finger down my chin, dipping down my neck, diving through my cleavage, all the way down my stomach to my pussy. He dips two fingers in me and pumps them into my vagina for thirty seconds, then slides them out.

I moan out my pleasure, even though he's not touching me anymore, his touch has been so savoringly sweet. Deliberate. Not seeming rushed by thoughts of others. Only me.

He's sucking his fingers, then there's a pop sound I assume must be him pulling them out of his mouth out while still sucking.

He says, "Mmmmm. Sweet." His voice is light and playful, but a bit more melodious than normal.

I almost giggle. Silly man. You know I taste sweet.

He's back dipping his fingers into my vagina and slipping his fingers up swirling them all over my clit to wet it, next squeezing my G spot and clit together with his fingers positioned both internally and externally. The dual pressure makes me groan big.

Another new move. I like it a lot. I need to mention that when we have our afterglow talk after this is all over.

He drags his fingers over the cleft of my pussy skin and back down again. He pumps his fingers into me for a few and then disappears.

Ruan Willow

I bite my lips together as I wait. Please come back quick Dane, Daddy Sir.

Out of the darkness, he touches my mouth, his fingertips prying themselves in, and I taste my salty-sweet self on them.

I roll my tongue around his fingers and then suck hard, my own taste flooding my tastebuds.

He withdraws his fingers out nice and slow, smearing my lower lip and chin with my saliva. His mouth crashes on mine as his body weighs heavily down on me. I struggle to breathe, but I don't want him to leave either.

I'm groping his tongue hungrily, gripping it with my mouth, sliding my tongue along his, then sucking it. Mmmm. Yes, there you are, lover. But something is mysterious. I should be spanked because now ... his tongue, his kiss feels ... different ... thinner yet more urgent in the dark. Somehow that kiss was stoked with a desperate passion I did not expect. I silently chuckle at myself ... whatever, I'm being dumb and ridiculous. What would make his tongue feel different? I'm a dumbass. I should tell him, so he gets to spank me again, though I'm a little sore from last round still. I touch my warm, smooth skin at the base of my throat as we kiss again. I taste something spicy on his tongue. He must have dipped into the taquitos and fresh salsa I

The Mardi Gras Unmasking

made for the party. I smile because I love to please this man's stomach as much as his cock. He dipped into that dish all afternoon I had to warn him to stop and leave some for our guests. He had just grinned and taken another bite.

He sucks my lower lip into his mouth and lets it slip out before devouring my mouth again with his, all insistent and open wide, yet all-encompassing, demanding, devouring. A forceful kiss that tingles me up and down all the way to my toes. We deeply kiss for a full minute before he retreats. He must be really horny because his tongue movements are really aggressive. But I like it. My left eyebrow raises involuntarily.

My chest heaves as I beg, "Please, please Daddy Sir, touch my pussy again."

He lays his full weight on me, crushing me into the bed as he pants. He sucks my right earlobe into his mouth. His head bumps my mask and almost throws it askew off my face. But I remain a good girl, keeping my eyes closed still. It makes me savor him more, not being able to see him, experience him.

"Oops," he says as he rights my mask. Even now his voice sounds different again in this drunken darkness. Kinda sexy as if it's someone else. The thought ruffles up my lust to near explosion.

Ruan Willow

I silently chuckle. I'm a fool though LOL. He sure would laugh at me if I told him I thought he was someone else. That's naughty yummy and total fantasy fodder.

I moan as he trails kisses down my neck from my ear to the top of my right breast. I stretch up to touch his sides, but he firmly pins my hands back to the bed.

No touching now. Okay, noted, Dane. I'll play along with this plan for now. But I don't like it much.

He trails his tongue round the full globe of my breast, then snakes his way to my nipple. He licks my erect tit several times before he attacks it full on, sucking it into his mouth determinedly.

I writhe against his strong nipple, suckling, eating up all his attention. His hand grabs at my pussy.

Finally. I yell out a moan.

Three fingers in, then he drags his wet fingertips up to molest my clit with my wetness.

I grasp up for his face blindly in the near darkness, but he flings my hand away. My lip droops out. Oh, pooh! I want to shove my hands into his lush hair and grab it, pull it, but I will have to grab fistfuls of sheet instead because I'm not supposed to touch him. I don't like this game. I gasp and grind my pelvis

The Mardi Gras Unmasking

against his hand until he lets out this low guttural sound which belts out more primal than hunger.

His mouth leaves my tit as he thrusts his boner into my pussy urgently, his sudden burst of aggression a nice little surprise. Oh, what wonderful passion! I love this round, Dane! I giggle.

He rams himself into me so fast; he is grunting and groaning, making new sounds I've never heard him make before, his breath rampant in his rage fucking of me. I'm thrashing my head back and forth as I fall into my orgasm like I plunge off a tall cliff. The ride down is so delicious as I curl my body upward in response to my climb. My orgasm causes my vagina to squeeze his cock, convulsing several times as my climax finishes. He groans and pounds harder. After five pumps, he jerks himself out of me and my belly is splashed with the wet warmth of his cum.

Well, that was quick! I stifle my giggle with my fist in my mouth, biting my fingers instead of belting out a laugh. It's not his usual to be so quick.

He breathes on me, his breath coming in rapid pants splatting against my face in hot puffs, his chest heaving as just the top of it presses against me. I imagine his cum squishing

Ruan Willow

across our bellies, sandwiched between us as he settles himself, his body heavy upon me. I nuzzle my face against his hot sweaty skin, finally touching skin-to-skin, solidifying the mutual bond of our pleasure. I smile. Our lust just meshes like water on water.

I keep my hands from roaming, per this round's annoying as fuck rules. I roll my eyes, geez. Must each round change the rules? Damn. I'm itching like fuck to caress him. Our breathing is raging fast, almost in unison, though his is more ragged and forced from all his heavy thrusting into me. He did all the work, and I got all the pleasure. Well, so did he LOL. My skin must be glowing, beaming it out into the dark … love love love being pampered sexually by him. He loves to do it, so we match up. I never, ever imagined myself as a sub. I used to think subs were weak women. Boy, was I stupid. Still speechless, I let out a slow sigh as I calm back down to baseline, floating down, the most blessed of queens nestled between my man and the bed.

He kisses my forehead and drags a finger down my cheek before climbing off of me, his aroma of bourbon and vanilla intoxicating my drunkenness further. I must remember to ask him what he put on. He smells delicious. I know as usual we will save our small talk for the end.

And then he's gone, just as quick as he came.

The Mardi Gras Unmasking

"Please come back," I whisper. The desperation in my voice is almost embarrassing. I crank down on my urge to tear up. I refuse to cry.

He taps my shin and whispers, "Will."

"Oh, shit, I thought you left." Damn, a good thing I didn't cry, I would have ruined this moment.

After a minute of laying naked on the bed with my eyes still closed, he says, "That was awesome, baby girl stroking up my cum like that with your hungry cunt. Keep those eyes closed until you hear the door close, okay, sweet cheeks?" Dane's voice thankfully sounds Dane-like again.

"I will, Daddy Sir." I nod to show I am a good girl, and I will listen, even though he probably can't see me. I will listen in this role play with you Dane, my Master, my Daddy Sir, that is. But … in normal everyday things, no bossing me around. My eyebrow raises instinctively. He gets it and he gets off on me letting him boss me during sex, and I'm not telling a damn warm or frigid soul about it. It's our secret. My skin still tingles from my orgasm, my throat very choked from gasping and groaning nonstop, but I feel invigorated too. Our sex has been phenomenal, unmatched, exhilarating tonight. And he's coming back for more. I can't wait!

Chapter Five

The door clicks and I whip my head to stare at the wall. I allow my eyes to fall closed again even though I'm so curious, desperately wanting to watch what he will do next. Super quick turnaround time with him back already. Fuck yeah.

"I'm back," Dane says in a hearty, thick, husky voice full of lust. "You can open your eyes; the lights stay off though."

He hands me something and I sit up to take it. I finger it. It's a shot glass and a wedge of lime. I sniff the glass. "Tequila?"

"Yes," he says emphatically, no impatience, just matter of fact. "How do you feel?"

I down it and hand it back empty as I suck on the lime. I giggle as I cringe, a weird sensation to do both at once. "It's so sour. But gave me a nice jolt." I smile easily. "I feel amazing. Thank you. Hey, you remember the last time I drank tequila?"

He scoffs, which turns into a cough. "Do I? Umm ... hell yeah, I do. You stripped off your shirt and bra and gave me a blow job right at the bar at Mister's. Much to every man's enjoyment. And you made me come in front of all of them." He

The Mardi Gras Unmasking

takes my hand in his and kisses each knuckle before releasing me. Such a Prince Charming move.

"Yeah, I was a little schnockered. Felt like I was a porn star, I guess." My mom would kill me if she knew.

"You'd make an amazing porn star, baby. With those tits and your ass. Your beautiful face and pouty lips. Maybe you should consider a career change." His laughter sounds so joyous I can't possibly get mad at him.

I lay back on the bed and flop my arms out at my sides. "No thanks. Though tonight I'm feeling a bit like a porn star with all this delicious sex."

"You are doing perfectly. Now close your eyes for a minute and a half before you open them again. Count it out, Kara baby." The commanding tone of his voice wets my pussy, especially when he gets stern like this, or mad like he did yesterday when he handcuffed me to the bed and he made me cum so hard my body felt like I had slept for eight hours. I shudder, practically drip.

The glow from under the door and from the numbers on the digital clock illuminates the room. A sliver of light coming through the curtains flickers as the curtain dances from the vent below. I close my eyes as instructed to, like a good girl, as the music still pumps into my ears. Someone yells from time to time, but the sound I notice most is the rapid beat of his breath as he leans over me like he's still panting from fucking me, it sends shivers through my body.

I hear a zipper unzipping and flinch. I thought he was wearing shorts that slip on and off. Did he change? Oh tequila, you are messing with my brain. Unless … no he wouldn't. Would he do a switcharoo on me? My upper body twitches, my shoulders curl as I freeze in place. What if he is giving me someone to fuck? My clit spasms hard. I'd die. My breathing increases to full-on panting.

"I'm gonna fuck you hard. You're my whore right now," he says, and this time he sounds normal so my doubts, dare I say my hopes, are squashed. "My cunt slave bitch pussy fuck. I'll use you to come after I make you come. You better come good for me, kitten. Want you creamy."

My pussy wets at how he calls me "whore". It makes my clit dance again in a giant twitch. "Mmmm," I murmur. "Fuck yes. Fuck my pussy, Daddy Sir. Fuck it. Ram it with your majestic rod, Daddy. Rub those veins along my pussy lips, against my vaginal walls, and just fuck me. I'm your whore to use." I mewl like a kitten as I squirm about the bed, my head

The Mardi Gras Unmasking

swimming with want. My pussy throbs, brittle with a yearning for his touch again, even though I just had him in me, on me. This fucking escapade has me in a rage. Fuck, I'm horny intensified. "Just fuck me, Daddy. Fuck me good and nasty."

"For sure, you're my bitch."

I love you, my nasty-mouthed man.

He trails his fingers up both of my legs, stopping at my pussy to graze my labia lips, to pet me deliciously upon my clit. He gives my pussy a spank and I screech. He takes a turn dipping fingers from both hands into me before dragging the wetness up to my stomach to my nipples, where he spans both at once and then pinches them, pulls them as I groan, and arch my back, cringing when he tugs them to the point of pain. I lurch and squirm, push on his arms, but they don't move. Give me that pain I oddly love. Mmmm. Damn!

He yanks my nipples upward sharply, roughly.

I gasp, then whimper. He intends to rip them off my body. I grab the sheets on either side of me and squeeze the fibers with all my strength. I might actually rip them. I'm yearning for his mouth on my nipples. The pressure in my gut mounting. I need him to suck my tits. Please. I want to scream

Ruan Willow

out, "Ravage me, Dane! Suck my tits." But I can't form

as he chews on my nipples.

Finally finding my voice, I beg, "Please, suck my nipples,

please, please, please," I plead even though he's already sucking.

I can barely breathe. "Don't stop."

But he does. He comes off my nipples and slaps both of

my breasts.

I gasp and recoil, rolling away from him. Holy fuck me.

My fingers instinctively flex outward, almost to the point of

pain. Take me, Dane. He reaches for me and slaps my nipples

again. A shockwave travels through my body, blistering out of

my pours with each moan.

"Mmm, fuck," I mutter as I thrash about on the bed,

keeping my arms low. Never did I ever think that would feel as

good as it does.

He slaps my chest again and I writhe on the bed as I

struggle. My nipples are stinging but the softness of this bed. I

imagine an ooze spills out my pussy as I feel a shift inside. It's

probably a real ooze coming from deep within me from the last

time he fucked me, I'm so damn sloshy down there, downright

soupy.

The Mardi Gras Unmasking

He crashes his open mouth on my left breast and sucks so hard like he's milking me like those machines that suck milk out of cow udders. I moan and whimper. Fuck, it feels so good. He damn near might make me orgasm from just nipple play. That would be a new sensation. I want it.

"Uh. Use me," I mutter in a soft voice that turns into a moan. My pussy flares as I speak.

He grunts as his hand fondles the lower part of my right breast, my nipple in his mouth, his other hand massages my left tit, molesting it, squeezing it as I try to wiggle away but can't. My nipples are on fire, they are so hard and tender. He keeps chewing, sucking. Mmmmmm. My moans sound foreign, like I didn't make them but from a damned dementor.

He suckles both breasts in turn, my nipples now starting to hurt a little, He licks me in a straight tongue swipe from my cleavage down to the cleft of my pussy mound. He takes a long cleaning lash of my pussy three times in a row before pushing his tongue into my vagina. He grabs my ass cheeks hard, harder than his usual grip, and I jump at the deepness of his growl. My tummy is set aflutter with jittery butterflies. His aggression raging, terrifying, and thrilling me all at once.

He presses lightly on my clit with a thumb, then he applies more pressure as he eats me out. I moan and flop against the mattress as he licks across my swelling clit. He's making my clit swell on her way to rise up.

He molests my nipple again, hard. He bites it and instead of screaming out, my to-do list pops into my head. I need to wash Dane's work pants and my scrubs, and clearly, these sheets will need washing after all this messy sex. I need to call my sister and mom and dad. Then there's cleaning that needs to be done. I need to plan meals for the week and shop. My nipple is so hard it hurts, stuck between his teeth as he clamps down. Damn. That's gonna leave a mark. I feel dizzy and aroused all at once.

His mouth works over my tit, his lips gently kissing my areola snaps me out of my thoughts. Mmm. Wow, Dane. Never before has he spent this much time sucking and beating up a single nipple. Was that subspace I always hear about? Like my brain shifted from the pain. Like holy fuck, I think I hit subspace. My eyes go wide. That was crazy as shit. Dane will be so pleased when I tell him after.

I whimper-moan as he rides his tongue all over me. The skin between my legs stinging as his stubble scrapes my pussy lips as his face rides along. I'm crawling but going nowhere

The Mardi Gras Unmasking

through sheer ecstasy, rolling against my moans, filling the air, mingling with the song wafting through the bedroom walls. His stubble has come early this time. Usually, it's not until the morning. His stiff coarse chin hairs lightly repeatedly grazing my skin again sending waves of shivers to my clitoris.

He climbs around and lies next to me, pulling me on top of him. "Sixty-nine," he whispers in a voice hardly his own in the darkness. There is something delicious about that.

This request reminds me of how I sucked his cock in the alleyway by the grocery store the other night, my tank top pushed down over my nipples, my skirt sliding up to bare the bottoms of my ass cheeks, hovering just above the dirty rain-soaked ground, my grocery list held against his thigh so I wouldn't lose it. He had demanded I suck his cock and I am learning as a sub I must pleasure him as he pleasures me. My knees had screamed agony as they kneaded the pebbly blacktop as I bobbed my head on his boner. I had ignored the pain because I wanted him in my mouth. Like I needed him in my mouth. What a naughty thrill. I imagined the excitement of being caught by a horny man who would watch us and stroke, peeking around the corner like a horny lech, damn near coming myself.

Ruan Willow

My heart pitter-patters as I maneuver myself inverted to his body. He shoves his nose into my butt crack. He open mouth sucks as much of my external pussy flesh into his mouth as he can, flicking his tongue expertly at my skin folds and clit like a windsock on a strong wind. I grow weak. I need to join in.

I take the head of his cock in my mouth hungrily and ride it up and down, trying hard to not gag as I take him deeper into my mouth. My body lurches and jerks as I fall forward, accidentally causing his cock to stab the back of my throat. I gag. Ick …

He moans out deeply, which lessens the brutality of my gagging. I so want to please him.

I come off and giggle and he chuckles this chuckle that sounds less like him and more like his friend Jack.

I stop moving. Seriously? No, that's impossible.

I glance down at his thighs and in the dark, they seem slightly different than they normally do, somehow thicker. I scoff, almost snort. Stupid drunk me. Fuck, am I smashed or what? Ruined fucked drunk brain. Pretending he's someone else makes me wonder. However, if this were Jack … how damn delicious would that be? My clit twitches, something deep in my gut groans.

The Mardi Gras Unmasking

I silently laugh again as I re-consume his cock into my mouth, Jack or not, I'm going less deep this time, only taking the thick tip, but spending good time on his head, running my tongue along the ridge, dancing the tip across his taut skin. I suppress the urge to bust out laughing. This is Jack. I'm almost completely convinced and that really fucking thrills my socks off.

He slaps my right butt cheek as he sucks me and I flinch, then moan. What a delicious slap.

I slide my tongue down his cock and lick his balls, fondle them gently and I scoot forward to suck each one into my mouth in turn as he groans.

He draws me back so he can eat me again, crushing my pelvis to his chest with his strong hands.

His hunger is such a turn on ... fuck!

He whispers in a drunk brain voice, "Play with my asshole, wench."

I giggle silently. He doesn't normally like ass play much, except on me, but, okay, this isn't a normal night. If this is really Jack though, I'll just die because that would mean Dane is watching? I run my finger over the ridges rimming his asshole, running it along down his puckered skin to his butthole. I'm just a bit too drunk to be smart.

"Spit on my butthole, and shove your finger in," he murmurs again in that voice, the dark surely making the familiar unfamiliar.

Confusion consumes me, I widen my eyes. I've never spit on his butt before. He did on mine yesterday, maybe that is where he is getting this from. Either way, I like the idea of doing it. Which is odd but, whatever. When in Rome and all. I crawl to better position my mouth over his asshole and spit on him, destroying my smile to accomplish spit and rub my saliva all over his gathered skin before I assault his butt with my index finger.

He groans and thrashes, so I advance my finger deeper. I pump and lick all his skin all around my finger riding his ass. He groans and leans up to suck my clit hard in response, clenching my lower body hard against his face.

I might burst.

My body twitches and I lurch, my climax coming at me at lightning speed as he wildly face fucks my pussy. I mount the top of my climax, my finger still in his ass as my body pauses, then I tip over the edge, my body jerks causing my thighs to

The Mardi Gras Unmasking

twitch, rocking against his shoulders as I come once again. I'm panting, my whole body rocks in a series of bounces as my pussy keep contracting. I can't speak. My head falls onto his thigh as my legs try to scrunch up more, but can't so they curve up against his body, so my ass goes up.

"Mmm," he says in the quietest whisper as he stretches to catch my wiggling pussy in his mouth as I thrash about. "Yes. Yes. Yes. So delicious," he murmurs, his hot breath flooding my pussy. He sucks, slurping me all out as my body begins to settle. "Mmmm. Yum."

My voice is lost deep in me as he sucks my clit and I moan out and grasp at my lower abdomen. My clitoris almost hurts. I want to cry out, "Too much." I try to jerk away from his mouth, but he suctions his mouth to me more, restraining me to him with his strong arms, not letting me get away, holding my ass, forcefully crushing my pussy to his mouth. I groan out in a series of whimpers mixed with grunts. My finger slips out of his asshole as I attempt to roll away from him. He rolls me to the bed and hops off in like a single movement, superhero-like. I lay still, stunned as he lets out a guttural groan, followed by the sloshing on his hand of his cock. My body throbs but is at peace, like when I just worked out hard.

Ruan Willow

No creampie again? Oddest of oddities. He always creampies me.

He doesn't even move for like thirty seconds. My whole body still zings as I come down from the high, still shaking from the orgasm I remain still wondering what the fuck will he do now? He returns and grips my hips, turning me to my side, which causes my legs to align. I am frozen as my mouth gapes open. The pressure of his hands urges me to bend my legs up towards my chest. I give in, let his hands mold me.

"Hold," he commands.

Yes. He's still hard. Fuck yes. I so wish I could see his expression, but I obey as I grip my thighs and wait. The music in the next room gets louder and there are squeals and shouts. Something crashes and falls, sounding mostly like a body hitting the ground in a great thud. Probably, it's a man with how heavy it sounded. What a giant mess I will have to deal with tomorrow.

He tickles his boner at my pussy, and I can't help but sigh.

How is he possibly still hard? He must have taken a Viagra tonight. He did mention the other day that he was considering trying one out. And now, he's gifting me a new position. My mind reels. And how is he making this much cum

The Mardi Gras Unmasking

so fast? Whatever, it's a gift, Kara. Don't question it. It's my night. He said so.

Or this is Jack. A ripple jolts through my clit.

He kneels, butting his thighs up to me so our skin is flush. He uses his cock to spread my lips. He pumps, one hand on my hip, the other securing my thigh. He grips me hard for leverage and begins to thrust into me faster and faster as his body must have endless energy.

I wanna scream it's so good, but I moan instead as his skin slaps mine, sounding devilishly delicious. I'm gasping and moaning as he grunts and groans out. Mmmm his sounds are so good. Euphoria floods me, I'm here but I'm on the ceiling. I am nearing my climax once.

He yanks himself out of me.

"Mmm, fuck," he mutters.

He ejaculates on the bed, spewing his sperm out, wetting the comforter. I feel a pout coming on. Why didn't he just give me a creampie again? But he can't have much left in him anyway after all of this. I want to know more of what's going on, what this grand plan of his really is. I almost ask why, "why no creampie?" but I won't, it's because it's all happening as he planned. And the plan is, this is all for my surprise. I will obey.

Ruan Willow

He gets off the bed and I adjust my mask as being fucked sideways made it go askew on my face.

"Eyes closed, babe," he commands without allowing any doubt to permeate his voice.

I giggle. "It's so dark, anyway."

Dane says, "Just do it, my super sweet sub kitten." He touches my ass. It calms me.

I'm sure as a reminder he will spank me for not obeying though. I get it. He owns my butt, however; I want that. The thought makes me wet. Last week he took a Sharpie and wrote "Daddy's" across my breasts. I smiled all day long, wet as could be. I need that written across my ass next, in durable permanent marker. I want it in black ink, so it's obvious.

"Okay. Yes, Daddy Sir." I'm still drunk, or more like in a drunken sex stupor. I smile and silently giggle. This is surely high-level euphoria. I writhe on the soft bed. I'm so pampered by you, my amazing husband.

He gently gives my butt cheek a small slap. "I'll be back with a snack and another shot." He rubs my ass cheek and kisses where he slapped.

Phew. He's sounding more like himself again.

Chapter Six

I probably could get a lot of benefit out of a snack right about now, and not because I have the munchies. "Yes please." The door clicks closed. I raise my hand over my mouth as I pop my eyes open.

Immediately I am bored as fuck. What is taking him so long? I roll my eyes, twist my newly sized wedding ring round and round my ring finger. Tomorrow ... I need to do several loads of laundry. And I need Cheetos asap.

I smile into the darkness as I whisper, "Please bring Cheetos, Dane."

Fuck, I really want Cheetos so I'm going to say it, maybe my want vibes will reach him if I say it out loud. "Cheetos. Need Cheetos." Saying it three times should do the trick. Oh, yeah.

Tomorrow, yes, I will take the dogs for a walk while he works, then I assume we will grill our dinner, those steaks I thawed out. And then we will fuck for dessert unless we are too sore from all this beyond epic sex tonight. We can watch tv for a bit and sleep before work at the office Monday morning. A perfect day.

Ruan Willow

A crowd of people loudly argue out on the street, ending with a shrill female scream. I want to go look, but that would be breaking the rules. I'm to be bed bound unless otherwise told to move. One of the first rules Dane told me this morning over our coffee and egg sandwiches. We had foregone sex in preparation for tonight, and now I'm so glad we did that. I had begged for his cock in me at first.

I flop my arms on the bed, smacking it several times. I wanna scream. Should I get up and walk around, anyway? It sounds too difficult, though, and too risky. I might get caught. I press a fart out. Damn, I hope this stink dissipates fast. And damn, I need food. Double damn. I need his cock again, fricking nympho that I am. I need chips and cock, cock and chips.

Someone cackles, then sputters like he's dying in my living room. Is he okay? And what is that yelling? Sounds like a damn goat getting choked out there. I so want to go peek, but I know if I'm caught, I won't be sitting down tomorrow. Yet that might already be the case. I have no idea what Dane has planned next. I giggle, relishing the thought. I'd have to lie on my side cuz he'll spank me within an inch of my life.

"Hurry," I mutter. "Wait. Don't hurry, I still am stinky." I wave my hand across my ass to help the fart stink spread away

The Mardi Gras Unmasking

faster. I dash to the bathroom to pee quick, then zoom to the bed before I'm caught. I'm sure pee breaks are allowed. He's not that cruel.

I roll back and forth across the bed, touching every inch. I roll over to my bedside table and open the drawer. I dig for my rabbit wand vibrator and snatch it out of the drawer. I drop my jaw as I pant. I'm still so soaking wet, so no need for lube. I press the button and a little circle glows brightly beneath the pink rubber skin of the toy. I hold it on my clit and yell out at first contact. "Fuck."

I fall into a fantasy easy as a breath. Dane bending me over the edge of the bed and pulling my pants down to bare my ass. I'm commando as usual and he slaps my butt with his wide-open bare hand. My body lurches as my clit sends out jolts of electricity out to my body from the spankings. The lush slapping sounds his hand creates from contacting my skin, how I finger my pussy as he spanks me. How wet he makes me. "Mmmmmm." I roll onto my tummy and grind myself against the toy, my bare ass bobbing in the air. I almost am at the point of climax again when the door opens.

I freeze mid self-fuck.

Ruan Willow

"Ah, kitten. I see you got impatient. That's okay. I want you to feel good, come as much as you can. Your night here, babe. I hope you just edged though so I can make you come now myself." His mask catches the light as he looks back into the very lit up living room. "Turn your head and close your eyes until I say."

I switch off my toy and drop it to my side before closing my eyes and turning my head. I hear the door click shut, but I still wait for his instruction. Panting, I run my finger over my swollen labia.

"I have some cheese and crackers for you and some grapes. Plus, another glass of wine so why don't you have a little snack while I stroke myself watching your luscious body enjoy something to eat. Then we'll fuck again."

I scramble to my hands and knees and crawl across the bed to the tray of food. I can make out his form standing at the end of the bed because he's holding a lit tea light candle. He sets the little battery-operated candle on the tray. It flickers and the light dances around the many cupped sequins of his mask before he straightens up. My eyes fall down him as he strokes the lump at his groin. I reward his culinary treat offering by facing my ass

The Mardi Gras Unmasking

towards him as I peruse the food in the dim light. He easily strips his clothing off, his pants with the elastic waist fall to the floor.

"Mmm. Yes. Nice view, kitten. I'm gonna get that ass. Molest that pussy. Fuck you rotten senseless like the live blow-up fuck doll that you are." The light from the little fake candle flickers across his handsome face and body, illuminating his sculpted chest as he strokes his hard-on.

His degrading me makes my clit twitch as I pop a piece of cheese into my smiling mouth. I love it cause it reminds me how naughty-brained I really am. I shiver as the words "live blow-up fuck doll" repeat in my head. I sit and grab for my phone so I can light up the plate more to find a good cracker, the biggest hunk of cheese. I keep it pointed at the plate only, keeping my eyes there as I make a few cheese and cracker stacks. I pop one in my mouth and moan, flick my phone off.

"Mmmm. Delicious cheese and crackers. Yummy. Thank you, Dane. I really needed this. I'm drunk as a fucking skunk. Next time bring Cheetos too. Huh?" I giggle as I shove a grape in my mouth, after which I plan to take a generous sip of wine. "New bottle, right?"

"Yes. Freshly opened for you, sweetheart," he coos, his deep voice velvet and butter. He stops stroking his cock. His smile is gorgeous.

"You are so good to me. Love you." I pop another cheese and cracker stack in my mouth. The rich cheese is both tangy and savory, reminding me of our trip to the Wisconsin cheese shop when we were back home last month. This is probably the last of the wedge. I grin, remembering how mom had bought us two more blocks of cheese and surprised us on our way out the door.

"Love you too, baby girl."

"I think I may have hit subspace a bit." I take a mini bite of the cheese and spread its creaminess along the roof of my mouth with my tongue.

He freezes in place. "Serious?"

"Yeah, when you were going hardcore on my nipple. Like it hurt, but I drifted off. My mind went elsewhere to my to-do list. It was like I was here, but not."

"Whoa." He clears his throat. "I want to hear more about that later. That's unbelievable."

I sip the wine quickly to get the flavors of the cheese and wine together in my mouth all at once because it makes them both better. With a handful of grapes and one more cheese chunk

The Mardi Gras Unmasking

with a cracker against my palm, I crawl up the bed to the headboard, lean back against the back pillow I always leave there. I'm solidly comfy now.

"Want some snack too?" I ask as I insert two grapes into my mouth and chew, the juice bursting out sweet and lush against my tongue.

"Mmm. I'm good. I'll taste them from your mouth." He chuckles and then growls. "Watching you enjoy is driving me wild. I can never get enough of watching you enjoy yourself. You're my drug, kitten. Anything you do that you enjoy fills me up. I live to take care of you."

"How did I earn such devotion?" His words bathe me.

"Because you are so amazing and I love you." His hand is rapidly chugging along, beating his cock, the motion even in this dim light is unmistakable … he's edging.

I down several swallows in a row of wine, followed by another grape. I sip the wine once more. "And I love you and you are amazing." I beam my smile at him, sure he can't probably see my smile, but I don't give a fuck. I'm smiling. "Okay. Ready to commence fucking." I set down the glass on my bedside table and crawl to the middle of the bed to lie flat. "Need your love on my button, your cock in my honey pot."

Ruan Willow

He chuckles and turns off the tealight and we are swallowed back into almost full darkness. He crawls up the bed and hovers over me, as he lowers himself down, his cock flops on my belly first. He presses it into my stomach and its thick hardness nuts against my soft tummy so lusciously, it magnifies as he gently thrusts.

Fuck! I want him in me so bad. Rocking me, ramming me, thrusting into me like he's trying to touch my heart with the tip of his cock.

His open mouth falls on mine to devour me and I scramble to keep up with the aggression of his deep French kiss.

How is he still so hungry for me? I'm an inferno on the surface of the sun. I moan and grab his biceps, which feel puzzlingly heftier, but I'm digging in my nails. He's allowing my fingers to travel up him to meddle in the promised strength of his shoulders. We kiss for several minutes, me hungrily responding to his bold tongue thrusts and rubs.

He plucks my lower lip between his, taking it up into his mouth. He sucks it hard, rubbing his tongue along my lip. His lust rears as a bear as he rolls me over. With a wild slash, he swipes my hair to the side so he can trail kisses down my spine to the top of my ass as I arch my back. He travels my skin rapidly

The Mardi Gras Unmasking

all over my ass cheeks, licking and sucking, making hickies as he traverses, making his marks, ones I will wear with pride. And then he bites my right buttock.

I cringe, yelp, squeal as he bites me again. I squirm against his love bites on my bottom, grabbing the sheets into my fists as I moan. Another muffled yelp tears past my lips as he sinks his teeth into the back of my thigh.

His tongue dares deviance as he snakes it into my butt crack once and wiggles down towards my butthole.

I startle as he peruses over my back hold. I fight the urge to thrash away. My nerves pierce my calm. I'm losing myself again, but I'm still sticking to my ass fears ... fears that unfortunately persist even in my drunkenness as he pokes his tongue into my asshole. I fight every speck of the urge to scream "Get away."

He enters in too far and I freeze. My heart is pounding, my eyes go wide, I hold my breath. Panic rises up my throat.

I release my breath; my sigh helps me relax my shoulders. Maybe it's not so bad. It might be kind of ... erotic even. I force myself to loosen my shoulders as he leaves my rear, travels down to my pussy instead, and proceeds to stroke me from clit to anus with his tongue wide and flat. I roll my head, my smile lingering as he's so thoroughly savoring me. That's totally my favorite. "Make love to me, Sir Daddy, and fuck me too," I murmur. I moan and grind my pelvis up and down slightly as he bathes me further with his spit and tongue. Bless him. I can trust him not pressing what I'm not ready for. His honoring of my wishes brings tears to my eyes.

He crashes his face fully into my crotch as he sucks hard on my clitoris, his nose near my asshole.

I cringe slightly, but a wave of mounting my orgasm sweeps it away.

I cry out, my moans coming out way too loud. But who the fuck cares if someone hears me. I'm wildly thrashing about; my sounds flog the silent air in lush, unfurling shrieks as I tremble. I am a sex banshee, a vixen of goddess heights. My arms stretch across the bed. I might fly.

He grips my thighs hard with his fingers as he eats me out. I let out a small scream as he squeezes my clit between his upper lip and his tongue in a wiggling back-and-forth motion. He keeps it up, kneading my clit until I rage towards coming like a straight-line wind through previously still air, my groin ever seizing full and tall with lush sensitivity.

The Mardi Gras Unmasking

As I ride up my climax, my ass raises up and his mouth tracks my movements, never leaving my pussy as my body scrunches, rises, and lowers.

My legs bend and I yell out my pleasure as he slurps at me. My lips purse and my tongue protrudes out of my mouth as I finish coming hard, the kind of hard I almost hesitate giving in to at first because I know the intensity it will hurl me into. My clit commands her power. I fall victim to my body's reactions, my vagina wields her will with several contractions which in turn convulse out of my pelvis, traveling along my body like a radio signal before they slowly simmer down. I pant helplessly. Frozen in place, all movement seems too hard, but I recoil from his suck on my almost painful clit and I moan out a complaint. It's just too much, I can't take it, just … can't. I want to yell out … Stop … it's too sensitive. But can't … speak.

He lets my clit bits slip out of his mouth and I release the breath I had been holding in. He aligns my legs and rubs me from hips to toes in four full lengthwise movements with rough gripping hand strokes. I'm so floppy, it's luscious to be manhandled. He sucks the toes of my right foot, slithering his tongue between each toe before dragging it all the way up the length of my leg to my right buttock. He drags his hard cock

Ruan Willow

along my butt crack and rides his boner between my cheeks horizontally as he moans, his strong arms on either side of me, framing my body securely in his as he takes his buttjob. Cradled by him and his relentless pleasuring of himself, pleasuring me, I sink into euphoria once more.

I smirk. I'm not dumb. I know he's pretending he's fucking my asshole. I raise my butt up to present it better for him, my want for him raging me as I twerk.

He grabs our wedge sex pillow nestled at the headboard and taps me with it.

I raise up my hips so he can slip it under my pelvis, and I settle back down on it with my ass tipped up perfectly for him to optimally access me.

I love this fucking pillow. Literally, I do. It's one of my wedding gifts to him that has brought us much pleasure over the past year. A stellar buy. I bite my lip as I wiggle my ass, my lower belly brushing the velvet of the firm blowup pillow.

He turns on a flashlight and points it at my butt and spreads my ass cheeks. I squirm slightly under this limelight.

Oh, my Gawd! How weird. You've only seen my asshole probably five thousand times already, Dane! And where the hell

The Mardi Gras Unmasking

was he storing a damn flashlight? I giggle silently. I'm sure it wasn't his ass.

He pulls my arms back and slips our furry handcuffs on my wrists as I moan. Then he switches the flashlight off.

Oh, the flashlight was for the cuffs. "Mmmm. Yes, Daddy Sir, take me." My heart is pounding like prey, like the mad run of a wild deer being chased by a wolf, I am obviously the deer. And it makes my pussy flare for his wildness. We fall in sync beast to kitten.

He firmly grabs my wrists in one hand.

"I'm yours. Take me. Use me," I whisper into the soft comforter, with the intent of full submission.

He nestles the head of his enlarged penis against my pussy lips, rubbing it up and down several times.

Mmmmm. Fucker likes to tease tonight. His touch enraging me, I groan. My cheek is flush against the bed as he encroaches his cock along the backs of my thighs in preparation of penetrating me, sliding his shaft along me, touching my thigh gap as he rides himself into my sopping wet vagina. He rides me fast immediately from behind, groaning out his intense pleasure. He swats several spanks at my ass before stabilizing my hip with

Ruan Willow

his free hand as he thrusts himself hard into me, the exact way I like.

"Mmm, you like that, baby girl? Don't you? Mmm. Hmm. Gonna fuck you senseless." He rams into me like a bull as he mutters, "So tight. Fuck," he says in a very Dane-like voice, washing away my trepidation.

"Mmmm. Yes. Fuck me. Please fuck me. Mmmm," I sing out in a moaning voice. As he pounds me even faster, hard and furious like a raged animal, I chant, "Yes. Yes. Yes. Yes. Yes. Yes. Fuck me hard, Daddy Sir." My whole body jerks as he thrusts into me and my flesh jiggles everywhere he's slamming into me so strongly. And, oh, do I fucking love it!

I cringe as he gives a few more spanks to my already stinging ass with his open palm as his low growl grunts out, piercing the otherwise quieting air. Where has the music gone? Somehow the heathens in the living room have managed to turn down the music. I imagine the whole room of people just chill now, sitting on couches, chairs, against pillows, sipping wine and eating the cheesecake I made, or asleep.

"Yes," he whispers before he slams into me so hard like he's shoving me down into the middle of the mattress, each pound a fresh slap on sore skin.

The Mardi Gras Unmasking

But nonetheless, my orgasm builds, or perhaps because of it.

He suddenly slows and leans forward to grab at my breasts, pinch my nipples as he thrusts. He grunts and raises up off me then speeds up his pumping, pressing my lower back over my cuffed writs with his hand for increased leverage.

I raise my ass up as much as I can. I'm almost about to top out on my orgasm again when I sense him about to release inside me. He slides out and comes on my ass. Hot cum splatters my skin.

"Wow," I say, drunk on endorphins as they swim around lusciously with the alcohol in my body. I almost feel like I'm drowning in dreaming. I close my eyes and sigh deeply.

He kisses both of my ass cheeks and then he's gone.

"That was wild," I whisper into the dark air that perhaps has no ears.

But he clears his throat. "Yes, it was. You did phenomenally well. So proud of you and I've never seen you look more beautiful." Dane then whispers before he removes the cuffs, "Close your eyes, okay? Baby girl, I'll be back." He wipes my cum-streaked ass with a towel.

Ruan Willow

Chapter Seven

Sleepy, yet feeling high, my mind rolling about enjoying all the pleasure he has given me this evening. It's all so unreal, dual, like I'm somewhere else, like above, but down here, watching, yet still in my own body soaking up the pleasures and all the climaxes, fuck so many. I'm just getting fucked rotten, but I want it. I roll and end up on my back near the tray so I can grab for more grapes. I'm amazed his thrusting didn't shuck this tray right off the bed, he was so wild. I finish all the grapes and the cheese and crackers too while I wait for him to return. I scroll Twitter on my phone and comment here and there on friends' posts. Then I visit Instagram and I'm almost falling asleep when I hear the door click open. The door lets in light enough for me to ascertain he's carrying a lit tall fat candle in a jar and a bottle of champagne.

I love his sweet attempts at being romantic, especially after all this rough sex. What a gem he is.

He sways a slight bit as he walks, and the candle's flame shifts.

I grin as I notice the bag of Cheetos nestled between his thumb and forefinger. This man gets me. And melts me. I

The Mardi Gras Unmasking

scrunch up my shoulders and my nose, curling my neck as I watch him approach, juggling all this stuff. My tummy tumbles delightfully, just as it did when we dated. He hasn't lost his touch.

He tosses me the chips and sets down the candle on my nightstand. The candlelight flickers on his devil mask, lighting it up like its own party. Finally, some more light in here. He's been a trooper wearing that mask all night. Well, same for me, I guess. The partiers outside our bedroom door are so loud again, and the music blares. I imagine they are all duly as smashed as I am. Probably as horny too, with swollen bits and big raging cocks, trembling lips. They are boasting a second wind and all. I stifle a chuckle as I feel energized too.

"What's going on out there? It sounds like a damn orgy." I pop open the chip bag, squeezing it and making it make that obnoxious pop sound as it bursts open. The cheesy aroma mixes with the alcohol scent wafting off his body. Or off mine. Either way, I'm drifting in its deliciousness.

"They've all gotten a recharge with pizza. And yeah. Not far from an orgy out there, actually. There are a few fucking already in plain sight. Of course, Shane and Lana are going at it. The usual." He snickers as he unwinds the wire holding the

Ruan Willow

champagne cork in. "I could see a massive orgy happening very easily." He sets the bottle on the corner of the bed and works on wiggling the cork out with his palm over it as the safety.

"We should go join," I whisper. An orgy is another fantasy; I so want that.

"No, I want you all to myself right now. I know you want multiple partners though, don't worry I bet soon you will be okay with it."

I almost laugh. "Oh, I want very much to do multiple. Just," I pause. "Working it, mulling it over in my brain. You know I'm terrified of that desire of mine." Or have I already done it? I snicker and bite my lip. A girl can wish.

He nods as he works the cork fully out of the bottle. It pops out into his hand and a spray of champagne-tinged mist puffs out. "Oh, we will both work on getting you to your fantasy goal of a gangbang. I have no doubt about it at all." He directs his gaze to my bedside table. "Your wine glass empty?"

"Yep," I say as I slip off the bed to grab my glass and carry it over to him as my brain sinks into luscious thoughts of a multiple partner encounter. I sway as I meander towards him with a grin.

The Mardi Gras Unmasking

He laughs with joy. "Be careful, you are a bit wobbly." He takes the glass from me and then pats the bed. "We will just share this glass. I didn't have enough room in my hands to carry one, plus, I'm a bit drunk too so didn't trust myself."

"Yeah, I'm pretty sure we can share spit. We've been doing it all night." I giggle as I hover my nose over the bubbling champagne. I take a sip and the bubbles of the cool citrusy liquid pop on my tongue before I swallow. "Your stamina tonight is astounding, by the way. You take something?"

"Yes." He drops his clothes to the floor, making a soft thump.

"Wow. It clearly works. Holy fuck. You are like a damn bull in heat tonight. And I am a very lucky woman." I hand him the glass and he takes a giant gulp. "You are supposed to sip champagne, not chug it."

"I know." He sets the bottle on the small towel I keep on my nightstand. "I'm a glutton though, remember?"

"It's really good. Thank you." I must be beaming, my cheeks sporting a healthy rosy sexually satisfied glow. I hold my cheeks in both palms and savor the warmth radiating off of them.

He hands me the glass and I take another sip before he gently gathers my body to his in an embrace.

"Oh, don't I know it, you are the definition of a glutton," I say with assurance.

He releases me, takes the glass, and sets it on the dresser. My eyes are glued to him, love watching him move. "You are so good. How can I not devour you excessively? Madly? I want to taste you with champagne on your tongue and out of your pussy."

My eyebrow raises instinctively, "Mmm. I'm so in."

"I'm going to be in and fuck you rotten senseless, you horny bitch," he says in a strong stern voice which gives me delicious chills.

"Yes, Daddy Sir. Do me." I lick my lips as he sways the two of us back and forth as one.

"My precious, fucktoy. I need to get towels. Be right back." He takes a step backward and pats the bed. "Have a seat and gorge yourself on champagne before you topple over without me here to hold you up."

I laugh heartily. "I want you to topple me over."

The Mardi Gras Unmasking

"Oh, I will. There is like a zero chance of that not happening, believe me." He laughs, securing that I have nothing to worry about.

It's true. I'm his in all ways. It's how we both want it.

His skin shimmers whitish in the yellow glow of the candle, his mask catching candle rays in all its many sequins as they reflect and dance the light about. He nods at me and switches on the tealight candle.

"Rarrr," he growls. "Can't wait to lick champagne off your body. Been waiting for this."

The thought of his tongue traveling me sucking champagne off my skin sends a twitch through my clit. How luscious and decadent. I squeal as I sit down on the bed and swallow another mouthful of champagne. "I'm gonna have one hell of a hangover, all this sex, and booze."

"I'll bring you orange juice and honey on soda crackers and fix you right up then, my sex goddess." He disappears into the darkness near the bathroom. "It's my mission to pleasure you," he calls across the room.

I stumble along the bed edge to the bedside table to top off the glass, concentrating very hard to not spill as I do my best to get the bottle near the glass rim. I clink the glass on the bottle.

"Oops." I pour super slow to fill it and still manage to go too far so I have to take a sip before I pick it up. "Oopsie. I'm a klutz here spilling."

Soon I'll be drenched in champagne, anyway.

He arrives out of the darkness with three thick towels. He lays them on the middle of the bed, so we have a layer of terry cloth triple-thick above our comforter. Spreading them with care, his firm sexy body glimmers in the flickering light, his muscles rounded in all the right places.

"Think three will do it?" He smooths the triple-layer of towels out flat and pats it. "Put your lovely bottom right here."

"You are clearly soberer than I am because I just don't give a fuck. I just want you to fuck me again," I slur, then grin at my goof.

"Oh, baby girl, that I can promise you. I'm gonna fuck you so hard."

"I can suck it off you too." I situate my body on the little towel mattress.

"We'll see. First things first. Lay flat and spread your legs for me, my princess kitten cumslut. Your skin is getting a champagne bath, followed by my tongue bath." He pauses.

The Mardi Gras Unmasking

"Hey, can you stand on your own? Maybe we can do this in the shower?"

I flop my head to the side. "Nopey. I'll need help to stand."

"Nah. Never mind. Let's stay here. I'll give you a good ol' mattress pounding."

Oh, thank Gawd he said that. I cannot stand anymore, this I know. Champagne always hits me hard and fast. Raging horny and drunk, I'm a useless wanton slut.

He walks over to the champagne glass, stops. "Wait, let's shift you so your pussy is near the champagne. Easier access."

I roll off and he repositions the towels. I smile as I catch him eyeing up my ass. I maneuver back on and he spreads my thighs apart fully opening up my pussy to the air. I giggle in my excitement.

"I love your giggle, kitten baby girl. This is my pampering gift to you. Get ready."

In the candlelight, I notice a Q-tip between his fingers. He dips it in the champagne and hovers over my clit as my eyes widen.

I gasp as he rides the cold champagne-soaked cotton tip over my clit. The firm pressure he applies to my clit with the Q-

Ruan Willow

tip makes my body jerk. He removes it and teases my clit several more times, causing me to flinch and moan out with each touchdown.

I gasp and moan more as waves of pleasure radiate from my groin.

He rewets the Q-tip and advances the tiny head into my pussy before riding the hard tip of it up my lips to torment my sensitive clit again.

I jerk with each application of the cold tip, the little head driving me wild. He knows right where to press. I thrash back and forth against the touches and swipes. Like he's painting my pussy, the artistry of him who knows my pressure points, him cultivating the masterpiece of building my orgasm. He's a pro.

He dips it into the champagne again and spreads the cold wet tip across my clit, then sucks it off as I moan.

"Secret agent Q-tip torture?" I ask in a whisper. I'm loving finally having more light to see him this round.

He chuckles. "Something like that. It working?"

"Oh, fuck yes. Driving me wild."

"I could kinda tell, just kinda," he says in a full snicker. "Happy Anniversary. Well, almost anniversary." His love for me thick in his words.

The Mardi Gras Unmasking

"Happy almost anniversary," I mirror in a super sappy lovesick voice.

The champagne is cold as it hits my chest, streams plunging immediately down my cleavage to my tummy. I cringe as the coolness travels down all my valleys, dropping quickly off my sides. He pours it on my neck and the cool bubbling liquid flows rapidly over my breasts and abdomen. My nipples harden against the cold champagne, areolas crinkling hard to their fullest constriction. He sets the bottle on the bedside table and begins to lick the champagne off of my neck, the humps of my breasts, carrying his tongue slowly over my nipple where he swirls his deft tongue around the tip making it harder. He nibbles at each of my tits and I squirm away from him with a giggle and a moan. He gathers me back, slithers his tongue down my cleavage, and proceeds to tongue bathe my belly and my belly button, licking, sucking, kissing, cleaning, savoring me in this start of our lovemaking. He travels his mouth over my hip bones and across the tops of my thighs to my pussy as I gyrate along with his strokes, our foreplay to fuck dance in full bloom. I might as well be on a boat for my body undulates hypnotically against his mouth and hands.

Ruan Willow

He leans over me, grasping the champagne bottle. He holds the cold glass against my pussy.

I tremble and scream. "Fuck! You trying to kill me?"

He chuckles and quickly takes it away.

"Oh, my gosh," I exclaim, trying to catch my breath. "Fuck me, that was cold." He just erased all his progress.

"Can't help it. I love to make you squeal. Make you react." He presses the bottle to my thigh.

I shiver. "Brrr. Now you need to warm me up."

"Please…Daddy Sir," he sternly reminds. Dane shoots me a look, the Dom look, he's perfected it all too well already, which makes me smile and my desire rage, gripping me deep in my gut.

His chastising me flares my lust. "Please Daddy Sir, warm up my pussy."

He pours the champagne on my pussy mound and I gasp then scream as it dribbles down along my lips, oozing, dripping the frigid champagne past my cleft to cool my vaginal opening. It makes me squirm and jerk as it streams relentlessly along my skin.

The Mardi Gras Unmasking

I thrash my body about as it dribbles down my ass cheeks to the towels below my buttocks. "Oh, my Gawd, that's so cold! And that's not much of a warmup."

I'm clutching down toward my crotch as he smacks my hands out of the way.

"Oh, I'll heat you. Don't touch until I tell you too."

Yes. He's in charge of this show. I give him a slow grin.

He takes a swig of champagne from the bottle and sets it on my bedside table. He returns to my pussy and tosses his mask onto the bed beside me. He spits a mouthful of champagne at my pussy.

I scoff. But at least it's warmer from being in his mouth than directly from the bottle.

He proceeds to quickly lap it up off my pussy lips, taking each one into his mouth to suck, then slurping with his tongue up towards my clit. He dives his mouth and I moan out. He sucks me hard and begins to shove two fingers inside my vagina, managing to lusciously rub against my G spot with his fingers shaped in a curve.

I grab at his hair and intertwine my fingers, squeezing wads of it down to his scalp as I whimper and whine out my pleasure. Finally, so grateful, I get my fingers in his lush thick

Ruan Willow

hair. I can't stop writhing about, it's impossible to lie still between the cold champagne and his hot mouth.

He comes off my clit for only a moment so say, "Come for me, baby girl, angel-cunt-pie. One last time. Can you come for me? Come, baby, come. Come for Daddy. I'm going to lick you until you come."

He suctions his mouth fully on my clitoris, rolling his tongue against it in rippling undulations as I forcefully scream out my pleasure, unsure if I can come again, but yet, the rush of it seems imminent. He's relentless and his mouth massages me with his face crammed to my pussy so hard I wonder how he can breathe.

The familiar rise of my climax comes barreling at me and I explode into it with a punch, sending out convulsions from my clit, through my vagina in a series of uncountable massive contractions. I think like maybe sixteen? This might be my record. My legs bend up as my feet curl towards my soles. I'm whimpering nonstop as I fall along the descent of my orgasmic climax. I'm panting, my tongue is sticking out of my mouth. I become more aware of myself and suck it back in.

"Oh, my fuck," I whisper. "That was huge. I totally lost control." I gasp as I close my fingers together, grabbing the sheet as my whole body continues to react. "Damn, I'm shivering. My whole body is throbbing."

He wastes no time, and his cockhead is lined up at my vaginal entrance. He manhandles my bent legs upward, snugging my knees closer to my armpits, opening up my pussy wide for him.

I recover enough to run my hands up his arms, across his shoulders, and down his hard rounded pecks. I swipe at his nipples with my fingers and pinch them both as he penetrates me with a massive groan.

"Yes," he murmurs. "Mmmmm, fuck your pussy feels so good. Fuck yes. Been edging so long I'm gonna blow."

He thrusts into me slowly for a bit before he speeds up. Minutes go by as he gently rocks himself into me, deliciously caressing me deep inside where I can never touch. Then he thrusts hard. He's hitting me with such force I gasp, my clit starting to stand up, to thicken already with his fast pounds. He smacks his body on mine on repeat.

I moan and whimper and fill the air with rounds of yelps as he fucks me hard, splitting my world apart.

I'm slipping into almost passing out as he flips me over and fucks me prone doggy without any assistance from me. I am

Ruan Willow

floppy as a ragdoll. I plummet into the squishy realm like I'm dreaming, falling, feeling weightless as my brain shoves me down into a drunken sex coma. I settle deep in its lushness as the room darkens.

Chapter Eight

I wake up, still feeling a bit drunk. I gaze around and feel for Dane in the darkness. He switches on the lamp on his bedside table and reaches to roll me toward him on the bed.

"I slept?" I blink, trying to focus on something, anything in the semi-darkness.

"Yes. It's six in the morning now." He pulls my body flush with his.

I sigh. "Fuck. I slept like I was dead." I fling my hair over my shoulder to my back.

"You crashed after we fucked." His voice comes out so cool and calm, matter-a-fact. "I think you may have even passed out before I came."

"Oh my gosh. I'm just speechless, Dane." I sigh, snuggling into him as he cuddles me snug to his warm, hard chest with his arm. The smell of his skin is fresh, brisk like the ocean breeze liquid soap in our shower. I imagine my own skin must be still sticky with champagne and saliva. He kisses my forehead and I figure right now I must still glow. "That was

Ruan Willow

beyond amazing last night. I felt like I was drugged, I was so delirious. High on booze and orgasms. You literally ruined me. Thank you. You are such an amazing husband. I'm so lucky." I pause to bite my lip. "It was pure ecstasy. Just, wow, so fuck wasted on orgasms." I breathe in the scent of his skin again, can't get enough of my man. Corny as hell, but damn true. "An unforgettable night."

His face is beaming. "And lots of booze." He laughs. "Yeah. You sure got royally fucked from every angle, my baby girl." He pauses. "By them. Then me. Hot as fuck." He peers down at me as I gaze up into his deep chocolate brown eyes. They are happy, amused eyes. "Surprise. Happy Mardi Gras and anniversary." He laughs, waves his right hand in the air as he rubs my back with his left.

"What? Wait. Wait. Wait. Them?" I pause, raise my head further and tilt it to the side as I prop myself up on my elbow. "No ... it's true then? There were others other than you fucking me?"

He nods. "Yes."

"Them?" I repeat, rising up on my arm to gaze into his loving eyes. "Them who?" With a shaking hand, I press my

93

The Mardi Gras Unmasking

finger to my lips hard and flush so I can feel my teeth beneath before I speak. "I don't get it. I'm so confused."

He nods again. "Them. The men. They all wore my mask."

"Wait a minute." I sit on the bed with my legs crisscrossed, hands on my thighs. "No fucking way. You mean …you mean … I knew it!" I raise my fist in the air in a punch at nothing in particular. "My mind kept drifting, but I thought one time it was Jack. You had multiple people fuck me, didn't you? Did you give me a gangbang? That was the 'them'? Wasn't it?" My jaw drops, my eyes go wide, my lips gape as I stare. Simple and dumb, clueless as I ask, "A gangbang? No. I would have known. For sure. I totally would have." I pause, twist my neck for a better view into his highly amused eyes. "Wait. What the fuck? That really wasn't you all those times, was it? Was it Jack? Who else?" I shake my head as I watch a naughty grin grow across his face. My hand flies to cover my mouth. "Oh, my Gawd. Fuck. I mean, I noticed some differences, I wondered, actually hoped it could be true at times, but I thought I was just too drunk or clueless in the dark." I drop my hand from my mouth to my side. "Wait … what? No no no no. Not possible. You'd better explain now. How is this even possible? I'm not that stupid." I end my ranting hysterics with a wide-eyed stare right into his eyes. My anxiety rises up to scuffle across my throat, tightening it way too aggressively, making breathing difficult, like I've got two masks over my mouth. But the thrill of it is actually real and makes my heart beat savagely as my lips spread into a deeper grin. "You're enjoying this tirade of mine immensely, aren't you?"

His eyes are ablaze with enjoyment as he raises his left eyebrow, his mouth set in the biggest of grins. "I told you the evening was about you. Your reward and to fulfill your fantasy of multiple men. You let me play with you the way I wanted to — with the butt plug and we made great progress towards anal, which I'm very pleased about, so it was all about you last night. My grand plan worked out perfectly." He hooks my wayward curl behind my ear and lifts my chin to more squarely meet his gaze. "You've expressed your desire to do multiple, a sort of controlled gangbang or reverse harem, your fantasy. Or rather your confession." He laughs with pure delight. He loves my naughty desires. "But every time I've brought it up, you've shushed it out of fear. So, to prove to you that you can do it, I arranged it for you. In secret. Now you know you can do it." He clears his throat. "And we can do it again. You will do as I say,

The Mardi Gras Unmasking

with your permission always, and I will fulfill all your fantasies. We're a team." He traces a finger down my cheek and rubs his index finger all over my lips.

I lick his finger with a grin. He smiles back.

"And you know and trust all these men to leave them alone with me? That's ballsy, and I don't know that I like it." I stop stone-cold still as my heart forgets to beat and dread invades me. "Do I know these men?" I waver between being pissed off and feeling tricked, yet loving him for forcing me to live out my fantasy. "And you weren't jealous?"

He chuckles. "No. I mean. Yes. I mean … Okay, let's slow down. First off, I never left the room. See our corner chair there? I sat there and stroked my cock or stood to watch and edged the entire time they fucked you. I spoke at times to keep up the ruse. You were safe so no worries about that, okay? I loved watching you be pleasured to the peak of almost being comatose, in a reverie, a dream. I almost came every time you did. Well, once I did a little, but I wanted to edge, save it for when it was my turn to fuck you. And then I just let out a massive load too. As you probably remember. Or not because you conked right out." He strokes my hair and cheek. "My sweet girl."

Ruan Willow

"Wow," I say as the full realization settles in around my grumbling gut. I just fucked four men in secret and then him in a very short amount of time. "I pleasured that many men?" A delicious thought yet dumbfounded, I touch my pussy, which is quite tender now, though no longer puffy, but still sopping wet. "Oh fuck. It's like I knew, but I didn't. I just kept dismissing away all my doubts, assuming it was the wine, and that I was too drunk. Or it was the darkness tricking me." My hand flies up to cover my mouth once more. "Oh, my gosh." I giggle. "That was fucking awesome. I came so many times. I lost count. And it explains why you seemed so extremely hungry for me again and again."

"I'm always hungry for you. I can't get enough. And you made them all very happy, let's just say that. And if you want to do it again, as an aware partner, I'll set it up for you, gladly." He squeezes my shoulder. "Watching you get fucked turns me on. Watching you come multiple times turns me on. Immensely. And I'm the only one who gets to keep you in my bed for every day. So, I'm good with this." He chuckles and joy radiates from his eyes. "And every single one of them loved it and would happily do it again, lights on, or off. You pick."

The Mardi Gras Unmasking

I scoff, still overcome by disbelief bordering on excitement. "Holy shit. I can't believe you just did this. Really, you are amazing." My cheeks redden as I wonder … will I get to know who put their dicks in me last night, and how will I look them in the eyes without smiling a devilishly naughty smile?

"Kara, I love you, and I care about your sexual pleasure. Let's just say I'm obsessed with it. I will always ensure your safety, and yes, fulfill all your sexual needs and desires. I just want to be a part of it all. I want you to know I did this for you and only you. Well, and me because I rather enjoyed watching you get the socks fucked off you so much that you climaxed yourself into delirium. And then I got my turn last to play with you. It was perfection, my orgasm-soaked, booze-drenched wench." He laughs deep from in his belly. "Honestly, watching made me even hotter wanting to fuck you, if that is even possible, well, I didn't think it was, but clearly it is. With each guy who fucked you, my desire to fuck you myself flared brighter. By the end, I was raging so hard."

"You told one of them our sex signals … damn … you are good." I tip my head to the right as if that will help me process all of this. "But how did not a single one of them try anal?"

Ruan Willow

"Oh, they wanted to, trust me. Some asked. It was a part of the rules upfront. I told them your ass is only for me. And creampies too. They were all well briefed on the do's and don'ts. I was very clear and explicit."

"Oh." I shift my eyes back and forth as I remember someone slipped a finger in and a tongue more than grazed my butthole, twice. Thank fucking goodness he said that to them, though. I'm so not ready for anal.

"At least for penile penetration. I saw some of them play a bit with your bottom. I didn't stop them. I know your limits and I told them. They were respectful." He clears his throat and traces my right nipple, making it rise into an erect state again. "And the rule was if you had too much of something or they did something wrong, I would tap their shoulder. I told them all your safeword too."

I lay beside him again, my hand on his chest. I drag my finger back and forth across his warm moist skin, basking in our rehashing afterglow, my cheek nestled tight to his chest, my thigh propped over his. "And did you have to tap anyone?"

"Yes, when the first one was spanking you wildly, I tapped him after like five whacks, so he'd cool it. It was early on so if he spanked you too much, the others would not be able to

The Mardi Gras Unmasking

enjoy such action, nor you, most importantly, you … so I tamed him, pulled his aggression off a bit. He duly stepped back and apologized to me, and sent one for you, for losing control. He was a bit drunk."

I laugh with widened eyes. "Yes, that he did. Fuck, he so did. He started that pain train. My skin still stings from his slaps, well, and others after. I might be a bit sore for a while."

"You did beautifully, baby girl, my kitten cumslut."

"That was risky. I could have found out." How can I not smile at this man for packaging such an amazing surprise experience for me? So selfless of him.

He sighs with a hand raise. "Then, I would have just told you at that point if you called me out. But I also only let you touch the men who were built like me to keep up the mystery. If they had something on their body which would give them away, those were the hands-off men. Really, each one had different rules."

"I'm completely flabbergasted though. You've blown me away. I can't believe you let all those guys fuck me while you watched." Memories flood my brain of each man's touch and I shiver with excitement.

Ruan Willow

He squeezes me in a big bear hug. "No, baby girl, you've got it wrong. I let you fuck them. You got what I knew you wanted. Made sure." His grin is smug, sexy, strong. "In the dark and sufficiently drunk so your inhibitions were lowered, so you'd enjoy."

"And not notice the differences. Brilliant. Wow. I guess you're right. I mean, I wanted it, but I was too terrified to try, so you … just … did it." I nuzzle against his chest. "You fucking sexual genius, you." My trust in him thickens deep inside my heart. And I just know. He will always take care of my needs. Of me. My eyes sting with happy tears as I nuzzle against his chest. Don't want even happy tears right now.

"My pleasure is your pleasure. Our sexual needs are melding and I'm loving our new normal." He squeezes me once more. "I'm responsible for you, my sub's happiness and sexual satisfaction. As a Dom, this is now my goal. Always. Whatever you want, I will do."

"Are you sure?" My brain is still revolving around all that happened, oscillating, fixating on all those moments of extreme pleasure, of wonder, of doubt, of delicious pain mixed with the orgasmic gushes of panic and intense gratification as I fell fully into some of the most dreamy intense orgasms of my life.

The Mardi Gras Unmasking

"Yes, baby girl. Yes, I am." He kisses the top of my head over the part in my hair, his plush lips so comforting.

"I'm pretty fucked up in my desires, huh?" I could almost blush.

"Hell no. I'm finding new fantasies to fulfill through you." He snickers, his voice catching in his throat followed by a large exhale. He taps my head. "You got any other crazy ideas in there we can explore?"

"I'll snoop around my brain and let you know. I've got a few I can fine-tune and share." With our arms tight around each other, sleep seems imminent again. "I may wake up later wondering if this all happened or if it was just one kickass sensual erotic unbelievable crazy-ass dream."

"Real as real, baby." He presses his chin to the top of my head.

I could live in the warmth of this full-body hug.

"I'm going to need you to tell me who had their cocks in me tonight though. All our friends, right?" I allow a silent giggle to reverberate in my chest.

He laughs gleefully. "Yes. And I can guarantee you, the next time you see their eyes, you will know."

Ruan Willow

"Mmm. That's most likely true." I nuzzle into the warm skin of his chest and let sleep come near, fantasizing about who of our friends fucked me and if they will surely do it again.

"Oh, I know it." He kisses me on the lips, no tongue sneaking in. "Love you. Goodnight."

"Love you. And thank you."

I roll to my side of the bed and snuggle my pillow to my cheek, knowing full well the masks we all wear can also reveal our truths.

THE END

The Mardi Gras Unmasking

Ruan would like to thank all her fans (I wouldn't be where I am without you, love you!), her friends, and her family for all their support, and for the wonderful support from author BD Hampton and the audio guy.

About the Author

Ruan Willow is an erotica author, podcaster, and narrator. Her podcast is Oh F*ck Yeah with Ruan Willow on many podcast apps. On the podcast, she reads erotica, provides tips for improving sexuality, sexual health, and ideas to help improve sex lives within relationships and for solo play, including the reviews of sex toys, and she also conducts erotica author interviews. She has a website full of sexy stories at http://ruanwillowauthor.com where she publishes on a wide range of sexy topics. She is published on Literotica and is a proud co-author of the He Will Obey anthology, edited by Jay Willowbay that won the Silver Pigtails award for Erotica/Smut in 2021. She can be found on Twitter, Instagram, YouTube, MeWe, Tik Tok, and Pinterest. She loves sex, reading, cooking, pets, being outdoors, and spends a lot of time in her closet … because that's where she records all her audio! Please chat with her on social media, she really loves to connect with people.

Find Ruan here:

https://www.youtube.com/c/RuanWillow

http://twitter.com/RaunchyIs

http://twitter.com/RuanWillow

http://instagram.com/ruanwillow

http://instagram.com/ruanwillow1

http://instagram.com/ruanwillowauthor

http://www.pinterest.com/ruanwillow

https://mewe.com/i/ruanwillow

http://www.tiktok.com@RuanWillow

Other books:

He Will Obey, the Femdom Anthology: https://www.amazon.com/He-Will-Obey-Jay-Willowbay/dp/B08QFBMS9B/

Want Ruan to narrate your book? Look for her on the ACX website.

Ruan would like to thank her family and friends for their support and for the wonderful support from author BD Hampton.

Inside Ruan Willow by BD Hampton and Ruan Willow

https://www.amazon.com/Inside-Ruan-Willow-Between-Anthology-ebook/dp/B08YDKJ1XT/

Made in United States
Orlando, FL
21 February 2023